Dear Parent:
Your child's love of reading starts here!

Every child learns to read in a different way and at his or her own speed. Some go back and forth between reading levels and read favorite books again and again. Others read through each level in order. You can help your young reader improve and become more confident by encouraging his or her own interests and abilities. From books your child reads with you to the first books he or she reads alone, there are I Can Read Books for every stage of reading:

SHARED READING
Basic language, word repetition, and whimsical illustrations, ideal for sharing with your emergent reader

BEGINNING READING
Short sentences, familiar words, and simple concepts for children eager to read on their own

READING WITH HELP
Engaging stories, longer sentences, and language play for developing readers

READING ALONE
Complex plots, challenging vocabulary, and high-interest topics for the independent reader

ADVANCED READING
Short paragraphs, chapters, and exciting themes for the perfect bridge to chapter books

I Can Read Books have introduced children to the joy of reading since 1957. Featuring award-winning authors and illustrators and a fabulous cast of beloved characters, I Can Read Books set the standard for beginning readers.

A lifetime of discovery begins with the magical words "I Can Read!"

Visit www.icanread.com for information
on enriching your child's reading experience.

For Rob, who finally
got spectacles
—J.O'C.

For my sister Erica,
who sees us all
with such clarity
—R.P.G.

Re: Spectacles, the
otherwise wise Ms. Parker
was incorrectable.
—T.E.

I Can Read Book® is a trademark of HarperCollins Publishers.

Library of Congress Cataloging-in-Publication Data
O'Connor, Jane.
  Spectacular spectacles / by Jane O'Connor ; cover illustration by Robin Preiss Glasser ; interior illustrations by Ted Enik. — 1st ed.
    p. cm. — (Fancy Nancy) (I can read! Level 1)
  Summary: When Nancy's best friend, Bree, gets some glittery glasses to help her see better, Nancy, who likes to be fancy, wants to wear glasses too.
  ISBN 978-0-06-188263-0 (trade bdg.) — ISBN 978-0-06-188264-7 (pbk.)
  [1. Eyeglasses—Fiction. 2. Vocabulary—Fiction.] I. Preiss-Glasser, Robin. II. Enik, Ted, ill. III. Title.
PZ7.O222So 2010   2009020695
[Fic]—dc22   CIP
                                                                                                                             AC

14 LP/WOR 10 9 8 7 6 5 4 3 2   ❖   First Edition

Fancy NANCY Spectacular Spectacles

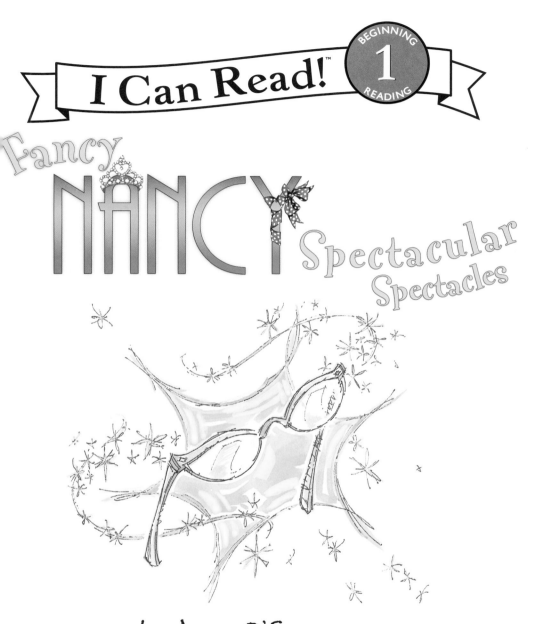

by Jane O'Connor

cover illustration by Robin Preiss Glasser

interior illustrations by Ted Enik

HARPER

An Imprint of HarperCollinsPublishers

Bree can't come over
after school today.
She is going to an eye doctor.

In school, her eyes hurt a lot.

It is very distressing.

(That's like upsetting—only fancier.)

I hope the eye doctor helps her.

That night,

Bree sends a note in our basket.

"I have a surprise," the note says.

I send back a note.

"Tell me! Tell me!" it says.

Bree sends another note.

"You have to wait until tomorrow."

I am not very good at waiting.

The next morning,

I race over to Bree's house.

Out she comes.

Bree is wearing glasses!

They are for reading.

Her eyes won't hurt anymore.

"Ooh la la!" I say.

"You look spectacular."

(That's a fancy word for great.)

Bree's glasses are lavender.

That's fancy for light purple.

And they glitter.

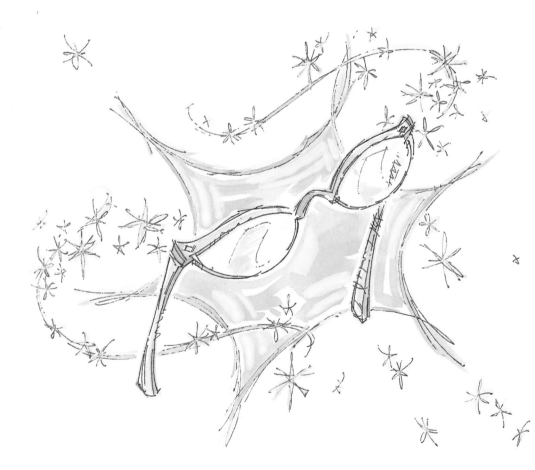

Bree puts her glasses
in a silver case.
Her glasses and case
are both so fancy!

At school,

Bree tells our class

about the eye doctor.

Bree had to read a chart

with lots of letters on it.

The letters went from big to tiny.

"Glasses are like magic.

I can read tiny stuff now," she says.

"Nothing looks blurry!"

"Your glasses are most becoming,"

Ms. Glass says.

That's a fancy word

I have never heard before.

Ms. Glass says it means pretty.

"I think Bree looks spectacular!"
I say.
Then Ms. Glass tells us
that spectacles is another word
for eyeglasses.
Wow! Bree has spectacular spectacles.

During math time,

Bree wears her glasses.

In the library,

she wears her glasses.

The eye doctor also gave Bree

a little silk hankie

for cleaning her glasses.

It is pink with purple polka dots.

I wish I had a hankie like that.

I wish I had a silver case.

Most of all,

I wish I had lavender glasses

with glitter.

Then I start to wonder.

Maybe I do need glasses.

At dinner,

I am pretty sure

my food looks blurry.

After dinner, I do a puzzle.

It has tiny pieces

and is very challenging.

(That's fancy for hard.)

I try squinting. Yes!

I do think everything

looks clearer now.

Later my mom comes into my room.

I am reading in the dark.

"That is very bad for your eyes!"

Mom says.

"I know," I say.

Then I tell Mom about Bree.
"I bet she'll get a fancy necklace,
like the one Ms. Glass wears.
It's not fair!" I say.
"I want glasses."

My mom does not get mad.

She says Bree has glasses because
her eyes need them.

"Your eyes are fine.

You are a lucky girl."

I know that, but I still want them.

Then I get an idea
that is spectacular.
My mom helps me.

My old sunglasses had only one lens.

So I popped out the other.

My glasses are just pretend.

But don't I look fancy?

Fancy Nancy's Fancy Words

These are the fancy words in this book:

Becoming—pretty

Challenging—hard

Distressing—very upsetting

Lavender—light purple

Spectacles—eyeglasses

Spectacular—great